Crystal's Christmas Carol

by Shirley Gordon

Pictures by
Edward Frascino

Harper & Row, Publishers

To Angela Perez Freedman
and Paolo Daniel Beaumont
with love

Library of Congress Cataloging-in-Publication Data
Gordon, Shirley.
    Crystal's Christmas carol.

    Summary: Vivacious Crystal shows a reluctant
Susan how to spread her Christmas spirit around when
the two entertain customers in a shopping mall with
a medley of carols.
    [1. Carols—Fiction.   2. Singing—Fiction.
3. Christmas—Fiction]   I. Frascino, Edward, ill.
II. Title.
PZ7.G6594Co 1989   [E]   87-33487
ISBN 0-06-022127-5
ISBN 0-06-022239-5 (lib. bdg.)

Crystal's Christmas Carol
Text copyright © 1989 by Shirley Gordon
Illustrations copyright © 1989 by Edward Frascino
Printed in the U.S.A. All rights reserved.
Typography by Andrew Rhodes
1   2   3   4   5   6   7   8   9   10
First Edition

"Merry Christmas vacation, Susan!" says
Crystal, as she pulls me into her room to show
me her Christmas tree. It has the longest

string of popcorn I've ever seen.

"I'm going to put it in the *Guinness Book of World Records*," says Crystal.

Sherri comes over from next door.
"Now we can practice our Christmas carols," Crystal tells me.

"I can't SING," I tell her.

"One little *fa-la-la* won't hurt you," says Crystal.

I give her one little squeaky "*Fa-la-la.*"

"Perfect!" says Crystal. "You can sing soprano."

Sherri *fa-la-la*s through a mouthful of Christmas cookies.

"You can sing bass," Crystal tells her. "I'll sing everything in between."

Crystal raises her arms like an orchestra conductor. "A-one, a-two...!"

"*Deck the hall with boughs of holly,*
Fa-la-la-la-la…"

"MEE-OW, MEE-OW, MEE-OW…" Crystal's
cat complains.

"He's a basso profundo," says Crystal.

Crystal grabs her father's old hat and we go outside.

"We're not REALLY going to sing in PUBLIC, are we?" I ask.

"*Christmas is coming, the geese are getting fat,*
Please to put a penny in the old man's hat...."

Crystal holds out her father's hat. She and
Sherri sing louder and louder.

"Sing out, Louise!" Crystal yells at me.

"My name is SUSAN," I yell back at her.

A Salvation Army lady is ringing her bell on
the corner, collecting money for the poor.
Crystal puts her father's hat back on her head.

"*Christmas is coming, the geese are in fine fettle,*
Please to put a penny in the Christmas kettle,"
she sings to the people going by.

"Thank you," the Salvation Army lady calls
to her.

"Merry *ding-a-ling*!" Crystal calls back.

"She means your BELL," I explain to the lady.

Crystal dances on down the block.
"Merry *boogle-de-boog*!" she hollers
at everybody.

Sherri dances along with Crystal.
"Catch the beat, Susan!" Crystal yells.

Crystal pulls me into a dance.
"Jitterbug, jitterbug,
Jitter all the way…"
Everybody stares at us.
Crystal giggles.
"Your face is redder than Rudolph's nose, Susan."
She dances into a shopping mall.

"Merry mistletoe!"

"Happy partridge-in-a-New Year!"

US MAIL

16

"Noel, all's well!"

"You have TOO MUCH Christmas spirit!" I tell Crystal.

Santa Claus is sitting on his throne in the middle of the mall.

"Take five," Crystal tells Sherri and me.

Crystal sits on Santa's lap.

"You look SILLY," I tell her.

"I never sat on a bowlful of jelly before," says Crystal.

"Ho-ho-ho," says Santa. "And what do you want from Santa Claus, young lady?"

"I want to know, ho-ho-ho, what *you* want for Christmas," says Crystal.

Santa's white cotton eyebrows pop up. "Nobody ever asked me THAT before."

"Christmas is for everybody," says Crystal.

Crystal hops out of Santa's lap and waves her arm at Sherri and me. "A-one, a-two..."

"*We wish you a merry Christmas,*
We wish you a merry Christmas,
We wish you a merry Christmas,
And a happy New Year!"

Crystal and Sherri march all around
the shopping mall.

*"Deck the mall with boughs of holly,
Fa-la-la-la-la...!"*

They sing as loud as they can. People come out
of the stores to see what's going on.

"Merry reet-bleet-a-coogie-oot-n-oo-DOW!"
Crystal shouts.

I try to duck behind the big Christmas tree,
but Crystal catches me.

"When you've got the Christmas spirit,
you gotta spread it around, Susan," she says.

"You spread it TOO THICK!" I tell her.

Crystal marches out of the mall and up
the street. She looks like she's leading a parade.
I drag along behind.

"O come, all ye faith-ful,
Joy-ful and tri-um-phant...!"
Crystal sings louder than anybody.
People throw coins in the hat.

"*He's making a list and checking it twice!*"
Crystal and Sherri call out.

Crystal leads her Christmas parade around the block. Colored lights twinkle on the rooftops. Christmas trees glow in the windows.

"He's gonna find out who's naughty or nice!" hollers Crystal.

The Salvation Army lady is still ringing her bell on the corner. Crystal pours the hatful of coins into the kettle for the poor.

"Bless you," says the Salvation Army lady.
"Christmas is for everybody," says Crystal.

I look around at the twinkling lights and the glowing Christmas trees. I see a smile on everybody's face. I feel a funny lump in my throat.

"We Three Kings of Orient are...!"
I start to sing.

When Crystal and Sherri stop looking
surprised, they sing too. We belt out the chorus
together in our biggest voices:

"O STAR OF WONDER,
STAR OF NIGHT...!"
"*Joy to the world, everybody!*" hollers Sherri.
"Merry   *boogle-de-boog*, friends and
neighbors!" hollers Crystal.

"HAPPY HOLIDAYS, UNIVERSE!" I holler.

Crystal gives me a squeeze.

"Now *that's* spreading it around!"